The Monster Snowman

by

Gillian Cross

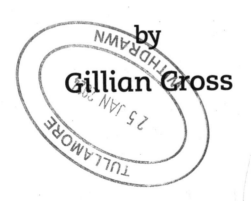

Illustrated by Ross Collins

First published in 2012 in Great Britain by
Barrington Stoke Ltd
18 Walker Street, Edinburgh, EH3 7LP

www.barringtonstoke.co.uk

ISBN: 978-1-78112-009-5

Printed in China by Leo

Contents

Chapter 1
Snow!

When Jack woke up on his birthday, he looked out of the window – and it was snowing! There was thick snow all over the road. Snow on the trees, snow on the walls, snow **everywhere**.

Jack jumped out of bed and ran downstairs. "Look outside!" he shouted. "I'm going to make a fantastic snowman!"

His mum grinned. "It's an extra birthday present!" she said.

"I hope you like this present too," his dad said. And he gave Jack a parcel.

Jack pulled the paper off. "Brilliant!" he shouted.

It was just what he wanted – a new phone. His old one hadn't worked properly for ages.

"I'm going to text Sam," he said. "And get him to come and help make the snowman."

"Not till you're dressed!" Mum said. "And you'd better wait till it stops snowing."

Jack went upstairs to get dressed. But he sent the text first.

Hi Sam, it said. Want 2 make a snowman l8ter?

Sam texted back right away.

YES!!! As soon as the snow stops. OK?

Jack thought it would *never* stop. But at two pm the last snowflake fell – and at ten past two Sam rang the bell.

Sam had a great idea.

"Let's go to the empty house on the corner," he said. "No one else goes there, and there'll be lots of snow. We can make a really big snowman there."

Jack pulled on his boots. "The biggest snowman in the world!" he said.

"The biggest, scariest snowman in the world!" said Sam.

As they walked down the street, they planned how to do it. But when they reached the corner, Ryan Stone was there, standing outside the empty house. He was looking up at the high wall that ran all round the garden.

"I bet there's good snow in there," he said.

Jack looked at Sam.

Sam looked at Jack.

Ryan was a wimp. He was scared of everything. If he saw them go into the garden, he would come too. They would have to let him. Or wait for him to go away. And they wanted to make a start on the snowman.

Ryan looked at the top of the wall again. "It's too high to climb," he said.

"Sam knows a way in," said Jack.

Sam sighed. "We're going to make a snowman in there," he told Ryan. "Want to help?" He went over to the big gate in the wall. It was made of long, solid planks of wood, running from top to bottom.

"I've already tried that," said Ryan. "It's locked."

"We don't need to unlock it," Sam said. "Look."

He bent down and pulled at the two planks in the middle. They were loose at the bottom and they swung to the side. The gap was just big enough to squeeze through.

"See!" said Jack. "Let's get going."

Ryan looked at the gap. "Is it OK to go in there? I mean – suppose someone catches us?"

"Stay outside if you're scared," said Sam. "We're going in!"

Sam and Jack scrambled through the hole in the gate. They hoped Ryan would go away, but he didn't. He dithered for a moment and then he climbed through after them.

Chapter 2
In the Garden

They stood at the side of the house and looked down the garden. It had a big open space in the middle, with trees and beds of flowers round the sides. And there was snow everywhere. The trees were full of it. The flowers were covered. And there was thick new snow all over the grass.

"We'll make the snowman right in the middle," said Jack. "Come on. We'll do the body first."

He made the biggest snowball he could and they started to roll it round the garden. As they rolled, it got bigger and **bigger** and **BIGGER**. When it was almost too big to move, they pushed it into the middle of the garden.

"Now the head," said Jack.

They rolled another snowball for the head. It was almost as big as the body and Jack had to stand on a heap of stones to fix it on. The snowman was taller than he was. It was taller than all of them. It was **massive**.

"It needs a scarf," Sam said. He found a long piece of ivy on the wall. "How about this?" He pulled the ivy off the wall and Jack lifted him up so he could tie it round the snowman's neck.

Ryan was down at the bottom of the garden, hunting in the rubbish heap. He came back with two light bulbs and an old brown bottle.

"Light bulbs for eyes!" he said. He reached up and pushed them into the snowman's face. "And can we do something with the bottle?"

Jack looked at the bottle. Sam and Ryan had both had really good ideas. But he wanted to think of the *best* thing. How could they use the bottle?

"I know!" he said. He took the bottle out of Ryan's hand and smashed it on a stone. The neck broke off and he stuck it into the snowman's head, below the eyes. "Look – that's a great nose," he said.

"Idiot!" said Sam. He looked round at all the broken glass. "What are you going to do with that?"

Jack grinned. "Teeth!" he said. He started picking up bits of glass and pushing them in to make a mouth for the snowman.

"Don't do that!" Ryan said. "You'll cut yourself."

"No I won't," said Jack.

But he did. He gashed his finger on a big piece of glass and blood came pouring out of the cut. It dripped on to the snowman, leaving a long line of red all down its front.

Ryan shivered. "Now he looks well scary!" he said.

Sam looked at the cut. "You'd better go home and get a plaster," he said.

Jack shook his head. "Not till we've finished the snowman. He's got to have arms." He wrapped a hanky round the cut and looked up and down the garden. "What about those two dead branches?"

They pushed the branches into the snowman's body, one on each side. Sam had brought his dad's big old gloves and he hung them on the ends of the branches, like hands.

"That's it," he said. "Now the snowman's finished."

"Hang on," said Jack. He'd just found something in his coat pocket. It was his old phone – and it had given him an idea.

"He can have this!" he said.

They pushed the phone into the side of the snowman's head and moved one of its arms up, as if it was holding the phone to its ear.

"Awesome!" said Sam.

"Fantastic!" said Ryan.

Jack took a photo of the snowman with his new phone. It was a spooky picture because the street lamps had come on. They gave the snowman's eyes an orange glow and glinted on its sharp glass teeth.

Sam laughed. "It's saying something nasty on the phone!"

"It's the best snowman in the world!" said Jack.

Ryan shook a little as he looked round the garden. There were shadows creeping over the snow. "I think we should go home," he said.

They began to walk back to the gate. But before they went they turned round for one last look at the snowman. It looked even bigger now, standing in the middle of the garden with its long, dark shadow stretching out towards them.

"It's amazing," said Jack. "Pity it has to melt."

They slipped through the gate and slid the planks back into place. Now the snowman was blocked from view – hidden behind the wall. It was their secret.

No one else knew it was there.

Chapter 3
I Dare You!

That night, Jack couldn't go to sleep. His cut finger felt heavy because his mum had put a huge bandage on it. And it hurt. He kept tossing and turning – and then he heard a text come in on his phone.

He sat up and read it.

Come 2 the snowman, it said. I dare u. S

The phone number was weird – it came up as %$&£!&%*&%*. But Jack knew the text was from Sam. It *had* to be. Who else knew about the snowman?

He got out of bed and peeped between the curtains. It was very dark outside. He knew his mum and dad wouldn't let him out so late.

But if he didn't go, Sam would think he was scared.

He took another look and then he started putting on his clothes. Very, very carefully, so he would make no sound. When he was dressed, he took his torch and went to the top of the stairs. There was a comedy programme on the TV downstairs and his mum and dad were laughing out loud. He didn't think they'd hear him.

He crept down the stairs on his tip-toes, crossed the hall and opened the kitchen door.

It was very cold outside. He wished he had his gloves. But he couldn't go back, in case Mum and Dad saw him. So he put his hands in his pockets and hurried down to the corner of the street.

As he reached the gate of the old house, he saw someone coming the other way. It was Sam. And he didn't look happy.

"You're crazy," he said. "Why did you dare me to come out here? It's freezing."

"*Me?*" Jack stared at him. "I didn't dare you. *You* dared *me.*"

Sam shook his head. "No I didn't. You sent me a text. Look." He held out his phone.

The text said –

Come 2 the snowman. I dare u. J

And the number was %$&£!&%*&%*.

Jack stared at it. "That wasn't me," he said. "It must be Ryan, playing silly games. Do you think he's in the garden already?"

"Yeah," said Sam. "I bet he's planning to jump out and scare us. Let's creep in. Then we can sneak up on him."

They went to the gate and slid the planks to the side without a sound. Then they slipped through the gap and tip-toed down the side of the house. They'd only taken three or four steps when someone came running the other way.

It was Ryan. He was looking back at the garden so he didn't see Jack and Sam. He squealed when he bumped into them.

"It's *creepy* in here!" he moaned. "Why are you trying to scare me? Where have you put it?"

"Put what?" said Sam.

Ryan glared at him. "You know what I mean! Where have you put the snowman?"

"The *snowman?*" Jack said.

"What are you talking about?" said Sam.

"Someone's moved the snowman," Ryan said. He was shivering. "It's gone!"

"It *can't* have gone," Jack said. He and Sam rushed to the corner of the house and looked down the garden.

Ryan was right. There was no snowman. Just an empty, flat space in the middle of the garden. And a line of giant footprints going round the far side of the house.

"I don't *like* it!" Ryan wailed. "Why did you make me come here?"

"I didn't make you come," said Jack.

"Nor did I," said Sam.

"Yes you did!" Ryan held out his phone – and there was the text again.

Come 2 the snowman. I dare u. J & S.

And the number was %$&£!&%*&%*.

Ryan waved the phone in Jack's face. "If it wasn't you two, then who was it?" he demanded.

Before anyone could answer, the ground started to shake under their feet. **THUD! THUD! THUD!** A huge shape came marching round the corner of the house. Ryan screamed when he saw it.

Jack couldn't believe his eyes. "That's impossible!" he shouted.

"It can't be true!" yelled Sam.

But it was!

The snowman was striding towards them, with its huge glove-hands held out as if it wanted to grab them. Its light bulb eyes flashed **ON OFF ON OFF** and its sharp glass teeth glittered horribly.

"Let's get out of here!" shouted Jack.

They turned round and headed for the gate. But when Sam tried to shift the loose planks, they wouldn't move! They were stuck. There was no way to get through the gate.

They were trapped in the garden. With the monster snowman coming to get them.

"What can we do?" wailed Ryan.

"Run!" yelled Jack.

Chapter 4
Monster!

They raced down the garden as fast as they could. The snow made it hard to run. Ryan kept falling over and Jack and Sam had to keep stopping to pick him up. Every time they stopped, the snowman got a little bit closer. His feet thumped down into the snow.

THUD! THUD! THUD!

"We've got to stop him!" Sam said. "What can we use?"

Jack looked round. There were three dustbins standing in a line against the wall. "Let's throw those at him!" he said. "Come on!"

They ran over to the dustbins and tipped the first one over. The lid fell off and all the rubbish fell out.

"Roll it!" said Jack.

All three of them pushed together and the dustbin went rolling over the snow. It crashed into the snowman's legs with a **THUMP!**

But it didn't stop him. He just lifted one giant foot and stamped down on top of it.

CRUNCH!

His foot squashed the bin as flat as a pancake. And he kept on walking.

"Try again!" shouted Jack.

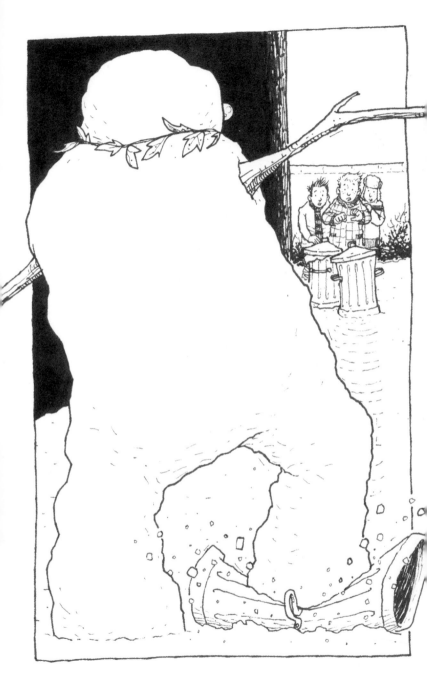

They jammed the lid down on to the second dustbin, so all the rubbish stayed inside. It was much heavier like that and it took all their strength to start it rolling. It rumbled over the ground like a tank.

But it didn't stop the snowman.

He lifted one foot and then another.

CRUNCH! CRUNCH!

The dustbin burst open and the rubbish flew out. It went everywhere. And the snowman kept on walking.

He was just a few steps away from them now and there was only one dustbin left.

"Let's *throw* it at him," said Sam. "Then he can't step on it." They all picked the dustbin up together and Sam counted. "One, two three – THROW!"

The dustbin went flying towards the snowman's body. But it didn't hit him. He lifted his huge hands and caught it out of the air. And he threw it right back at them!

"Duck!" yelled Ryan.

They all ducked just in time. The dustbin sailed over their heads and hit the wall. Rubbish flew everywhere and some of it hit the snowman in the face. He lifted his hands to brush it away – and that gave them a chance to dodge past him.

"As fast as you can!" said Jack.

They raced past the snowman and ran down the garden. They hadn't gone very far when they heard the **THUD! THUD! THUD!** of its feet coming after them.

"What can we do?" wailed Ryan. "He's going to catch us!"

"Don't be such a wimp!" shouted Jack. "There must be a way to stop him."

"How?" yelled Sam. "He's much bigger than us! There's nothing we can do!"

Jack looked into the darkness ahead of them. There had to be something they could use. But all he could see was trees and plants and snow.

Then he tripped over the garden hose. And that gave him an idea.

"Where's the tap?" he said.

Chapter 5
Water!

Sam pointed down the garden. "There! On the wall. But what good is a tap?"

"If we can get the hose going, we can spray the snowman with water!" Jack said. "And water melts snow, doesn't it? Come on! Hurry!" They ran down the garden, dragging the hose behind them.

The snowman was coming after them again. **THUD! THUD! THUD!** As fast as he could, Jack connected the hose to the tap.

"Bet the water's frozen," said Ryan.

But it wasn't. When Jack turned on the tap, a jet of water shot out of the end of the hose.

"OK, Mr Snowman!" yelled Sam. "Now you're going to get it!"

Jack pointed the hose at the snowman and the jet of water hit him full on. Right in his middle.

But he didn't melt. He was so cold that the water FROZE when it hit him. It turned into icicles – long, sharp daggers of ice hanging down all over his body. As he walked on again towards the boys, the icicles clattered together.

THUD! THUD! CLATTER! CLATTER!

Jack dropped the hose and ran on down the garden with Sam and Ryan on his heels. But when they reached the far end there was nowhere else to go. They backed into a corner, under a big old tree. And the snowman kept coming.

THUD! THUD! CLATTER! CLATTER!

"What can we do?" wailed Ryan. "He's going to get us!"

"Let's climb the tree," said Sam.

But they couldn't. All the branches were too high to reach.

The snowman was almost close enough to grab them. But it kept stopping and rubbing its body. It didn't like the icicles. They wouldn't rub off, so the snowman took hold of one and snapped it off. He threw it away – and it flew towards Sam.

"Watch out!" yelled Jack.

Sam ducked. The icicle went flying over his head and stuck into the tree trunk behind him. The snowman roared in anger. It started snapping off all the other icicles and throwing them as hard as it could. They zoomed through the air like arrows.

ZAP! ZAP! ZAP!

Some of the icicles dropped to the ground, but lots of them stuck into the tree trunk. All of a sudden, Jack saw they were making a kind of ladder.

"Come on!" he shouted. "We can get up the tree now!"

He started to climb, using the icicles like steps. Sam and Ryan followed him. They climbed up and up, until they were too high for the snowman to reach.

The snowman came to the bottom of the tree and looked up at them. Its eyes flashed. **ON OFF ON OFF**. It reached out with its great glove-hands and grabbed hold of two of the icicles. Then it lifted one foot.

"It's going to climb the tree!" Ryan screamed. "It's coming after us!"

Chapter 6

Spears

Ryan was in a panic, but Jack knew what they had to do.

"We need to knock the icicles down," he said. "To stop the snowman getting up here."

He snapped a branch off the tree and swung it at the top icicles. They fell out of the tree trunk and smashed down on to the ground, where they broke into tiny pieces.

"You have to help me!" Jack shouted to Sam and Ryan. "I can't do it fast enough on my own."

He leaned out of the tree and swung his branch at the bottom icicles – just as the snowman started pulling itself up. The icicles broke off and the snowman dropped back on to the ground.

Jack swung the branch again, aiming for the next two icicles. But he missed them. Instead of hitting icicles, his branch smashed into the snowman's arm. And some of the snow fell off it – leaving a dent.

"Look!" shouted Sam. "That's what we ought to do!"

He and Ryan broke off a couple of long, sharp branches. They began stabbing down at the snowman, using their branches like spears. Every time they hit its body, a little bit more snow fell off.

The snowman gave a great bellow of rage. Then it backed away from the tree.

"We've won!" shouted Jack. "It's going!"

But he was wrong. The snowman was just moving to safety. As soon as it was out of reach of their branches, it stopped. It bent down and scooped up new snow from the ground. It pushed the new snow into the holes in its body, patting and patting until the snow was as hard as ice.

When all the holes were mended, it lumbered back to the tree. But this time it didn't try to climb. Instead, it put its arms round the tree trunk and began shaking it. Jack and Sam held on to the tree, but Ryan nearly fell out. They had to grab his jacket to stop him crashing down to the ground.

"H-h-help!" he said as they pulled him back. "W-w-what are w-we going to d-do?"

The snowman shook harder and harder. Faster and faster. Jack's teeth were rattling and he knew he couldn't hold on much longer. He leaned out of the tree and shouted down to the snowman.

"Stop it! Why won't you leave us alone? What do you *want?*"

The snowman let go of the tree. It stepped back and lifted its great head to look up at them. "**COLD!**" it shouted, in a creaky, shivery voice. "**I'M SO COLD!**"

Chapter 7
What Do You Want?

The snowman's voice was so loud that the branches trembled. Jack put his arms round the tree trunk and leaned down as far as he dared.

"Of course you're cold," he said. "You're a snowman."

The snowman shook its great head from side to side, scattering snowflakes everywhere. The ivy flapped and its glass teeth clattered together. "**Co-o-o-oLD!**" it wailed. "**So VERY** co-o-o-oLD!" It looked up at them, with its light bulb eyes flashing.

"We're cold too," Sam shouted back. "We're just as cold as you!"

The snowman didn't answer. But it opened its mouth wide and its brown glass teeth glinted in the moonlight. It started to shake the tree again.

"You need something HOT!" Jack shouted in panic. "Like – like – " He said the first thing that came into his head. "Like fish and chips! And hot chocolate!"

The snowman stepped back again. It put its head on one side and looked up into the tree. "FISH?" it said, in a puzzled voice. "CHIPS?"

"That's very hot," Jack said.

"Steaming hot," said Sam.

"The hottest thing you can think of!" said Ryan. "Except hot chocolate."

"FISH," said the snowman. "CHIPS. HOT CHOCOLATE." It looked up into the tree and held out its huge gloved hands. As if it was waiting for fish and chips to drop down into them.

"There isn't any up here," Jack said. "You have to get it from a shop. With money."

The snowman shook its head from side to side. They could see it didn't understand. "COLD!" it said again.

"We could get you some fish and chips," Ryan said in a helpful voice. "If you let us out of the garden – "

That was a bad thing to say. The snowman gave a huge, angry roar and grabbed the tree again. It started shaking the trunk even harder than before.

"It thinks we're trying to trick it!" shouted Sam. "We've got to make it understand – "

Jack leaned out of the tree and shouted down at the snowman. "If you want fish and chips, one of us has to go to the shop. The other two can stay here. OK?"

There was a long, horrible pause. Then the snowman stepped back from the tree again. "FISH. CHIPS," it said in its scary creaky voice. "HOT CHOCOLATE." And it waited for one of them to come down.

"Hey – we need some money!" Jack said.

They all felt in their pockets. Ryan had a pound. So did Sam. Jack didn't think he had anything. But then he remembered the money his mum had given him for the school trip next day. That was five pounds. They'd have to use that.

He held it out – and they all looked at the money. Who was going to take it and climb down the tree? The snowman was standing at the bottom, looking up at them. Was he really going to let one of them out of the garden? Or was it just a trick?

Suppose he grabbed the one who climbed down?

Jack was so scared he could hardly breathe. Being up the tree was bad. But being grabbed by the snowman would be *much* worse. There was a long silence.

Then Ryan said, "I'll go."

"*You?*" said Jack. He was amazed.

"I've got to get out of this tree," said Ryan. "I'm scared of heights. They make me feel dizzy." He took the money and put it in his pocket. "One fish and chips and one hot chocolate. Right?"

"Right," said Sam. "And be *quick*!"

Ryan nodded and leaned out of the tree. "I'm coming down!" he shouted. "I'm going to buy you some fish and chips."

The snowman nodded and stepped back from the tree. It watched as Ryan climbed down. The moment he touched the ground, its great hands shot out and grabbed him round the waist.

"Help!" Ryan yelled. "Jack – Sam – HELP!!!"

But before they could do anything, the snowman lifted Ryan high into the air. It lifted him right over the garden wall – and dropped him down on the other side. Jack and Sam heard the thump as Ryan's shoes hit the pavement. Then they heard the sound of his feet, running away down the road.

Sam looked at Jack. "Maybe he won't come back," he said. "Maybe he'll be scared."

"He's *got* to come back!" said Jack. "Or we'll never get out of this tree."

They were very cold now. They turned up their collars and blew on their hands to try and warm them up. All they could do now was wait.

Wait and see if Ryan came back.

Chapter 8
Fish and Chips

The snowman kept walking round and round the tree, hitting it with his arm. Snow slid off the branches and fell down Jack's neck. He shivered and looked at his watch.

"It's no good," he said, after half an hour. "I don't think Ryan's coming back."

"Wait a minute," said Sam. "Listen. Can you hear someone running?"

Jack listened. Then he leaned out of the tree and looked up the road – and there was Ryan, racing round the corner! He had a parcel in one hand and a cup in the other.

The snowman heard him too. It went striding down the garden **THUD! THUD! THUD!** and tugged at the gate. The gate swung open and Ryan tumbled through it.

"Hurry!" said Sam. "Let's get out of this tree."

He and Jack slid down to the ground and ran up the garden. The snowman didn't even notice them. It was too busy looking at what Ryan was holding.

Ryan held out the mug of hot chocolate. The snowman reached out its great glove-hand and took it from him. It stared down it, looking puzzled.

"You have to take the lid off," Ryan said.

The snowman frowned.

"Like this," said Ryan. He reached out and took the lid off.

The snowman leaned forward and sniffed at the hot chocolate with its shiny glass nose. Then its mouth opened wide. The sharp glass teeth glinted as it lifted the mug to drink.

Jack and Sam crept closer to Ryan. "Give it the fish and chips," Jack whispered. "Put them in the middle of the garden – away from the gate."

Ryan walked down the garden. He unrolled the parcel of fish and chips and put it down in the middle of the empty space. In the place where the snowman had been in the beginning.

The snowman lifted its head from the mug and looked round, sniffing at the air. When it saw the fish and chips, a huge smile spread across its face.

"**HOT!**" it said in its icy, croaking voice.

It thumped down the garden and lowered itself on to the ground, beside the parcel. Putting the empty mug down, it reached out and scooped up a handful of chips.

"Time to go!" whispered Jack.

He tip-toed up to the gate and Ryan and Sam tip-toed after him. But before they went through they took a last look back at the snowman. It was sitting in the middle of the garden, with one hand full of chips and the other hand full of fish. They could hear it chewing loudly. **CHOMP! CHOMP! CHOMP!**

"It's really scary," Ryan whispered. "But it's amazing too."

Sam nodded. "But I still don't understand about those texts. If none of us sent them – *who did?*"

Jack looked at the snowman. It still had his old phone stuck into the side of its head. For a moment he wondered if ... But that was impossible! Wasn't it?

"Let's go home," he said. "I'm not coming back here until all the snow's melted."

Chapter 9

The End of the Story – or is it?

That night, it started raining and it went on raining for three days. By the time the rain stopped all the snow was gone. Jack and Sam and Ryan came out of school and looked at the wet grey pavements and the soggy green grass.

"Do you think the snowman's gone?" said Sam.

"We'd better go and find out," Jack said.

Ryan shivered. "Do we *have* to?"

"Yes," said Jack. "If we don't, we'll always be scared of that house. Come on. Let's go and look now."

They went down the road to the empty house. The gate was still unlocked and they propped it open with a stone. Just to be on the safe side. Then they crept along the side of the house and looked down the garden.

It was empty.

Everything was wet and green. There was no snow anywhere, but they could see a little heap of things in the middle of the grass. They walked over.

There was an empty fish and chip paper and an empty cardboard mug. A pair of gloves. Some broken brown glass, a pair of light bulbs and two long branches, like arms.

Jack looked down at them all. "So that's it," he said slowly. "The snowman's gone for ever."

They gathered everything up and took it down to the rubbish heap. Then they walked back up the garden. They were almost at the gate when Sam stopped short.

"Hang on," he said. "There should have been something else."

Jack and Ryan looked at him. "What do you mean?" Jack asked.

Sam looked back down the garden. "Where's your old phone? The one you gave to the snowman?"

They went back and hunted all over the garden, but they never found it.

And as they were walking home, Jack had a text on his new phone.

The number was %$&£!&%*&%* and the text said –

C u next time it snows ...

Our books are tested
for children and young people by
children and young people.

Thanks to everyone who consulted on
a manuscript for their time and effort in
helping us to make our books better
for our readers.